T0130553

# The adventures of

# Abby and the Seahorse

## B.I PHILLIPS

Copyright © 2021 by B.I PHILLIPS. 823878

All rights reserved. No part of this book may be reproduced or transmitted in any form or by any means, electronic or mechanical, including photocopying, recording, or by any information storage and retrieval system, without permission in writing from the copyright owner.

This is a work of fiction. Names, characters, places and incidents either are the product of the author's imagination or are used fictitiously, and any resemblance to any actual persons, living or dead, events, or locales is entirely coincidental.

To order additional copies of this book, contact:
Xlibris
844-714-8691
www.Xlibris.com
Orders@Xlibris.com

ISBN:    Softcover        978-1-6641-6001-9
         EBook            978-1-6641-6002-6

Print information available on the last page

Rev. date: 02/22/2021

GRATEFUL ACKNOWLEDGEMENT

To

FLORIDA POODLE RESCUE

And

NORTH DALE ANIMAL HOSPITAL

Abby: "Hi. I am Abby."

Seahorse in water : "Hi. I am a seahorse.

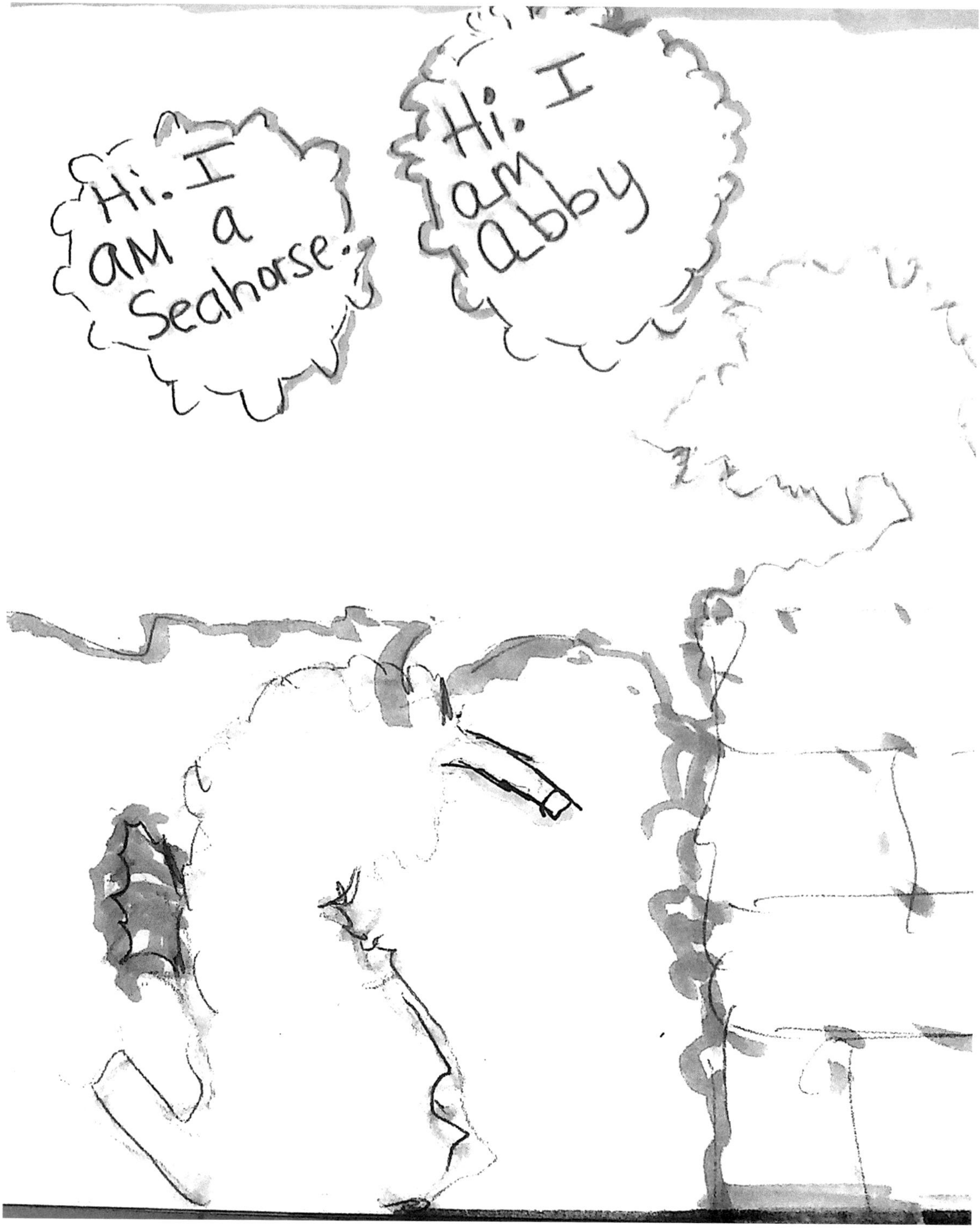
Hi. I AM a Seahorse.
Hi. I am Abby

Abby: "Do you eat with knives and forks?"

Seahorse: no we suck food up with our snouts."

Abby: "How do you stay warm?"

Seahorse: "We use solar energy and stay in shallow waters."

Abby: Do you have wars?"

Seahorse: "Only in Romance."

Abby: "Do you have jails?"

Seahorse: "No, we don't have jails"

Abby: "Do you have higher education?"

Seahorse: "No, we are all actors"

Abby: "Actors in terms of how?"

Seahorse: "We mimic the color of
underwater plants."

Abby: "we eat four basic food groups."

Seahorse: "We eat 3,000 shrimp each day."

Abby: "population growth?"

Seahorse: "Habitat loss."

Abby: "Do you have a president?"

Seahorse: "Whales rule the ocean."

Seahorse: "Today, I brought a friend. This is five the fish."

Abby: "Hi five, nice to meet you."

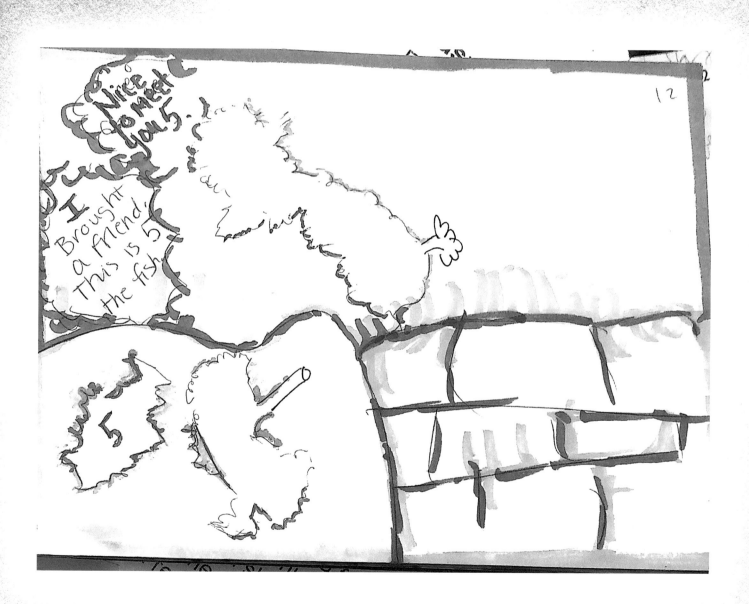

Abby: "Do you have viruses.?"

Seahorse. "we get ick."

Abby: "where is five the fish?"

Seahorse: "Swimming around"

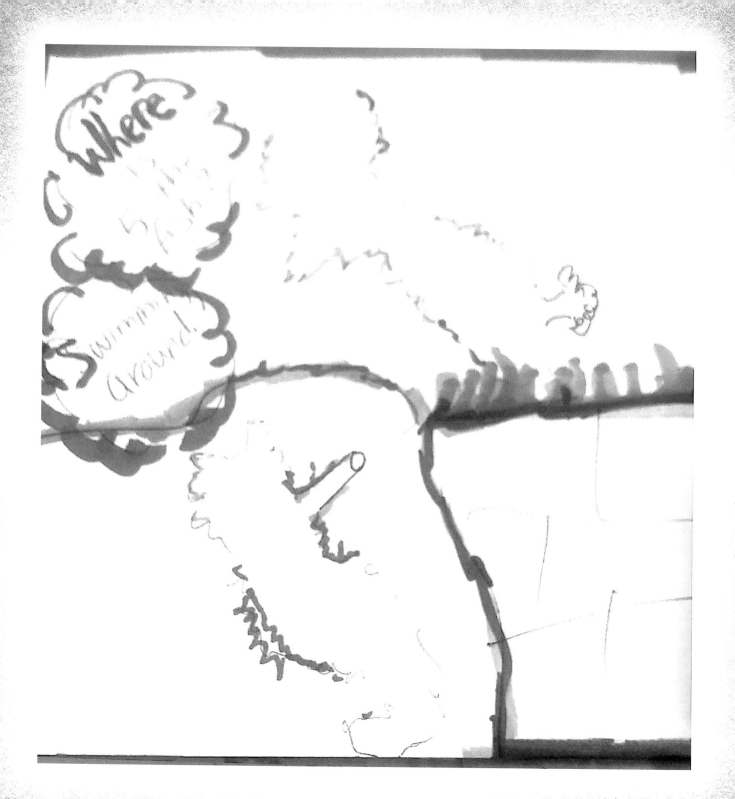

Abby: "Where do you live?"

Seashore: "Coral reefs and inlets"

Abby: "Do you have cars?"

Seahorse: " We use the fins on our back"

Abby: "We have the 4 basic food groups"

Seahorse: " We eat up to 3000 shrimp a day"

Five the fish: "I can't find the seahorse anywhere?"

Abby: "Where did you see him last?"

Five: "by the fishing docks."

Seahorse: "help us! I brought the ducks."

Run!

Get back here

That was a close call.

Thank you my friend

Your welcome

The end

Printed in the United States
By Bookmasters